THE SANTA CONTEST

Merry Christmas)

Ryan

From:

Mrs. Fry

Grade 4

If you like this book,
be sure to look for these other Apple Paperbacks
by Linda Ford:

Santa Claus, Inc.
Santa S.O.S.
The Santa Solution

THE SANTA CONTEST

LINDA FORD

AN
APPLE
PAPERBACK

SCHOLASTIC INC.

New York   Toronto   London   Auckland   Sydney
Mexico City   New Delhi   Hong Kong   Buenos Aires

ISBN 0-439-34449-2

12 11 10 9 8 7 6 5 4 3 2 1   1 2 3 4 5 6/0

Printed in the U.S.A.   40

First Scholastic printing, November 2001

In memory of my father —
Thanks for everything, Linda

CHAPTER 1

It's hard to say which day in my life has been the most miserable. I don't mean to sound pessimistic, and I really don't want to sound like I'm feeling sorry for myself. But lately I think I've had more than my fair share of lousy days.

Count them. There's the day I realized I didn't want to go into the family business and be Santa Claus but didn't know how I could get out of it. And there's the Christmas Eve I had to do all of Santa's job anyway. And I'll never forget the day Granddad disappeared, and we didn't know if he was alive or not.

And then there's the afternoon our long-lost relatives showed up. If they had stuck around for just one day I wouldn't have minded so much.

But their arrival started a long chain of miserable days, so you've got to put them all on the list of my unlucky days.

I had no idea what was waiting for me when the doorbell rang.

Everyone else was gone. Our family's florist shop was closed that day, so Dad was at the golf course. He wasn't any good at golf, and I'm not sure he really enjoyed it. But after he bought the clubs and took the lessons, he was too embarrassed to admit he didn't like it.

Mom was out exchanging Christmas gifts at the stores. The gifts were from her parents. It doesn't matter what Grandma and Grandpa give; it's either too small or too big.

My twin sister, Marcia, was at her friend's house where they were trying on each other's Christmas clothes.

We hadn't had a very jolly holiday. Granddad had the flu, and since Marcia and Dad were both sick, too, I'd had to make the Santa Claus rounds. What were the chances that they'd all be sick so I'd have to do it? I really have lousy luck. Everyone was feeling better by the day the relatives came, except me. It was going to take a while before I stopped having nightmares about getting airsick on the sleigh.

My three other sisters were with Mom at the store. They'd wanted to stay home with me.

Mom said, "Nick? Do you think you could baby-sit? I'll cut my errands short and get back before your movie."

I didn't answer her, just rolled into the couch and pretended to be really tired.

"Well, I guess not," Mom answered her own question.

"Come on, Nicky!" Brenda pounded on my head.

"Sssshhh, let your brother take a nap. He lost a lot of sleep over Christmas," Mom said, and then hustled them all out to the car.

It still amazes me when Mom falls for my act. I mean, she's pretty smart, for a grown-up, and you'd think she'd see through it.

Whether Mom was fooled or not, she'd still taken the girls with her, and that's the only thing that counted. I figured there were at least six years of favors that my folks owed me. Not that they agreed. Dad nearly frothed at the mouth when he saw the headlines about Christmas Eve and the mistakes I'd made as Santa Claus. But I'd done the best I could, and I wasn't going to beat myself up about it.

Merry and Christmas got up on the couch and

crowded in beside me. That's what I call the two strays I picked up on my Christmas Eve flight.

"Those are stupid names," Marcia had told me.

"It's like giving them half a name," Mom said. "If you have to call them something like that, why not call the dog Merry Christmas and the cat Happy New Year?"

"Because the cat is Merry, and the dog is Christmas," I replied, "and it doesn't matter if they only have half a name each, because they're always together anyway."

Mom sighed and rolled her eyes. Mom and Dad weren't thrilled about having more animals around the house. My sisters pick up kittens like they're collecting marbles, and Mom had finally declared they could have one kitten each. So she couldn't object to me having a cat. A dog was extra, but like I said, Mom and Dad owed me.

Merry and Christmas seemed to enjoy being my pets. They had been skinny when I found them, but now they were already fattening up. They slept on my bed at night. Somehow they always ended up in the middle and me on the edge.

As soon as the door closed behind Mom, I scooted Merry and Christmas to the side and bounced off the couch. I never liked naps. Mrs. Sandoval, my kindergarten teacher, used to get so upset.

"Nicky Martin, stop poking Jake and go to sleep!"

That was the biggest reason I got "unsatisfactory" in behavior.

Jake was my best friend ever since first grade. We didn't like each other before that, mostly because our moms tried so hard to make us be friends. Then when we were six, they had a fight and wouldn't speak to each other for a couple of months, so to bug them, of course Jake and I turned into buddies. Matt moved to town that year, too, and the three of us have hung out together ever since. They wanted me to go see a movie later, so I had about an hour to do whatever I wanted without my sisters in my way.

I'd just gotten into the best part of my new video game when the doorbell rang. It was probably Matt and Jake early, so I yelled "Come on in" and went to level five. The bell rang again, loud, and then there was heavy knocking.

"The door's open!" I yelled.

The bell rang several more times. Doggonit. I'd never gotten that far before. My concentration was shot, and I blew it on level six.

"Why didn't you just come in?" I asked, opening the door.

Oops.

It wasn't Matt and Jake. There was a man, big

and tall, with a red face and one of those "glad to meet you" grins. The woman was much shorter. Her hair was stiff with curls, and she wore lots of makeup.

"Uh . . . sorry," I said. "Can I help you?"

"You can if you're one of the Martins," the man said in the hearty voice my baseball coach uses when he's trying to get on the good side of parents.

"I'm Nick Martin," I answered. I thought they must be salespeople. Saturdays were always a big day for them.

"We're probably not interested in whatever you're selling," I said, starting to close the door.

"Whoa! Whoa!" the man protested. "We're not here to sell a thing. My name's Buck, and this here's my wife, April. And over there's our son, Steve, only we like to call him Rammer—on account of the way he plays football."

I hadn't noticed the boy who was standing off to the side, kicking the rock Mom had gotten Dad to haul up from the river for her. She'd planted things around it, and old Rammer was standing on top of them. Boy, was *he* going to be popular around here.

"It's, uh, nice to meet you."

I couldn't tell them Mom and Dad weren't

there. House rules: Never tell strangers that no adults are home.

"Good to meet you, young fellow. Are your parents home?"

I guess they didn't know the house rules.

"Mom's in the shower," I gave the standard line. "You'll have to come back later."

"That's just fine," he said. "You just tell your folks that some long-lost relatives came by and that we'll be back this evening."

Relatives?

"Are you, uh, Martins or Porters?" I asked. Porter was my Mom's name before she married Dad.

"Neither." He winked like we both knew a secret. "We changed our name back to the original. We're the Claus family."

CHAPTER 2

I stood staring at them as they drove away. And I had lots of questions.

The Claus family?

What did they mean by that? And what did that winking thing mean? Did they know about the family business? They couldn't, right? After all, they had to be a whole lot of generations removed, or we'd have known about them. And anyway, even if an ancestor had passed on stories about Santa Claus, Inc., they wouldn't take it seriously. I mean, who'd believe a crazy story like that?

The first thing was to let Granddad know. We have a special phone line that goes straight to the North Pole.

"Granddad — you won't believe who just left our front door."

"Visitors from the Black Lagoon?" he said, trying to be funny. Grandma and I are the only ones in the family who can *really* tell a joke.

"No. The Claus family," I told him.

"Very funny, Nick."

"I'm not joking! There's this guy and his wife and some kid they call Rammer who came and said they're our long-lost relatives, *and* they said their name is Claus."

"Claus? Are you sure?"

"They even knew we'd changed our name to Martin."

"Hmmmm. Did you say anything, you know, about the business?"

"Of course not!"

"Well, don't worry about it. I'll get security on it right away."

Matt and Jake came banging on the door about then, so I grabbed some paper and scribbled a note for Mom and Dad about the situation. Then I tried to forget about the whole thing at the movie theater. But I couldn't, not completely. I had a horrible feeling that something was about to blow up in my face.

*   *   *

9

We stopped for burgers after the movie. It was great to be on winter vacation. Snow was beginning to drift down on the way home; I wished it'd stick enough to go sledding, but sometimes we don't get that much where we live. Mostly that's good, since I don't want to shovel it.

"Hi, Mom!" I yelled when I walked through the door.

"Where have you been?" Marcia hissed from the stairway.

"In a galaxy far, far away, and then I made a visit to the Old West, and then . . ."

"Give me a break," she interrupted.

"I was at the movies. Mom knew about it."

"Okay, okay. But you'll never guess what happened. There are some people here, and they say they're related to us."

"Already?" I groaned. "It's only four o'clock. They said they'd be back *tonight*!"

"You mean you knew they were coming?" Marcia demanded.

"Yeah, I left a note."

"I guess Mom and Dad never got it."

"Son!" Dad said from the doorway loudly. "I'm glad you're home. We have visitors."

"Sure, Dad, but can I see you for a minute first?"

He walked away from the living room door

with a relieved look on his face. We ducked into the kitchen with Marcia. Mom was already there making coffee.

Mom waved a piece of paper. "I just found your note."

"Did Granddad call back about the security check on them?"

"No," she replied. "Here, take these cookies in, and I'll bring the coffee and cocoa."

I passed the cookies to the "relatives" while Mom and Dad poured coffee for the grown-ups and cocoa for us kids; I just took some cookies. Then I dropped into a chair and heard a really disgusting noise.

Pppplfffft.

The noise silenced the room. Rammer started laughing and so did his father. With every eye staring at me, I gingerly reached underneath my rear end and pulled out a whoopee cushion.

"Now, Rammer," his mother said in a kind of prissy way, "I told you to be nice to your new cousins."

"Oh, well, April," Buck said, red-faced from laughing, "it's all in the family. A good joke never hurt anybody, now did it, young fella?"

He winked at me. I tried to smile and pretend it was funny. So far, Buck reminded me of Stinko Jones, the most obnoxious kid at my school.

"Hey," Rammer announced, "did you see that game on Christmas Day? What a riot. The quarterback just rammed that ball right into a touchdown."

He swung his arm back and tossed a cookie clear across the room where it bounced against the wall. But as he released the cookie, his elbow knocked his mother's arm and her coffee sloshed over the side of Mom's new couch, the one Mom and Dad gave each other for Christmas. My sister Sandy stared at it and gulped.

"Oh, no!" Mom exclaimed, then stopped and bit her lip.

Buck was laughing again. "Happens around our place all the time." He looked at me. "Bet you're always pulling that kind of stunt yourself, aren't ya, buckaroo?"

Marcia's face was clouding up, like she was about to blow her top, but Dad gave a quick shake of his head, and Marcia bit her lip, just like Mom.

"Don't — worry about it," Mom managed to say. Not that either Rammer or Buck was worried.

April dabbed at the brown stain with a napkin. "I'm so sorry," she said. "But I'm sure it'll come out. Just use a little salt and soda water."

Mom nodded and smiled stiffly.

"Sure," Buck boomed. "Why don't the two of you girls work on it before getting dinner, while the rest of us boys go out to work up an appetite."

Underneath her polite mask, I could tell that Mom was shocked, so I guess she and Dad hadn't said anything about dinner; the new relatives had just invited themselves. And Mom was too nice to tell them to go jump in a lake.

"What d'ya say, Nick?" Buck asked. "Let's go show them how football oughta be played."

"Well, Mr. Claus," I said, "I'm — "

"Now, none of that. We may be cousins, but you just call me Uncle Buck."

"But — Uncle Buck," I began, "I'm really more of a baseball kind of guy."

"Ah, I'll bet you're pretty handy with the old pigskin. Now, come on, fellas, I'm not going to take no for an answer. And you pretty little girls," he beamed down at my sisters and actually patted Marcia on the head, "you four can be our cheerleaders."

Marcia looked ready to chew nails.

The evening only went downhill from there.

After "Uncle" Buck and his family finally left, Mom got the younger girls into bed, then Mom and Dad, Marcia, and I met for a family conference.

"Those awful people!" Dad groaned.

"They're not really related to us, right?" Marcia pleaded.

I told her, "Only if we're willing to admit being part of the Frankenstein family."

"Now, Nicholas," Mom said sternly, "that isn't very nice."

Mom hates it when we say bad things about people.

"Sure, Mom, but — "

"You shouldn't say things like that. It isn't fair. They aren't at all like Frankenstein's monsters. The monsters were — *much* nicer than that."

We all stared at her in shock. I guess Mom can tell a joke after all. Then her lips quivered and we started laughing. She leaned against Dad and laughed till her eyes started watering.

"It *was* simply *awful*," she said finally, wiping her wet cheeks. "Maybe we should sneak out of town tonight so they can't find us again."

"That's a good idea, Mom." Marcia giggled. "Maybe the Feds would let us into the witness protection program."

"Impractical," I told her. "The Feds are probably hiding from them, too."

"Well," Dad said, "there's at least one nice thing I can say about them."

"Oh?" Mom raised an eyebrow.

"It feels awfully good when they leave."

The next morning, Granddad called with the report from the security department. It was the worst possible news: Those people really *were* our long-lost relatives.

CHAPTER 3

Granddad was on the speakerphone. "So," he said, "this is unexpected, but it's nice to know there's more of us in the world than we thought."

"Wait till you meet them, Dad," my father groaned.

"Well, I'm looking forward to seeing them, I'm sure. I'll be down this evening, but I have to go back right away. Too much to do this season of the year."

Some people think Santa Claus's work is done by December twenty-sixth. But not everyone celebrates Christmas on the twenty-fifth; some Russians do it on January sixth, and the Ukrainians on the seventh, and the Armenians celebrate on the eighteenth, so Granddad had plenty more work to do.

"Uncle" Buck and his family showed up at nine o'clock.

"Howdy, cousin," he said to Dad, and held out his hand. Dad reached forward to shake it, and we heard a loud *buzzzzzz*! Dad jerked.

"Yeow!" Buck chortled, and Rammer snorted something you might call a laugh. "Quite a hearty shake you've got there."

Dad was rubbing his hand where the joy buzzer had got him. I guess Rammer learned his jokes from his dad.

Sandy, Brenda, and Teresa got to go upstairs and watch television, but Marcia and I were stuck doing the company thing. Sometimes it's a real pain being the oldest.

After a few minutes, Buck leaned back and yawned. "Hey, Toots," he asked Mom, "is that coffee I smell?"

"I suppose there might be some left from breakfast."

"Breakfast! Boy, that sounds good. Got any bacon?"

"No, but I could make you some oatmeal," she replied.

Buck grimaced and changed the subject. I guess he doesn't like oatmeal. "Well," he said, "it's

17

sure great getting back with the family. We've missed out on a lot."

"Yes," Dad answered stiffly, "we've gone in different directions, I suppose."

Different directions was an understatement.

Now, I'm the first to admit that my family isn't perfect. They don't have much sense of humor. Oh, Mom and Dad make lots of jokes, but until last night I'd never heard either of them say anything really *funny*. And when it comes to certain things, especially Santa Claus, Inc., they don't always listen too well. It took forever for them to understand I was really bad at being Santa and that Marcia was really good.

I guess I could list a lot more faults, but even with those, Mom and Dad aren't that bad. After meeting the Claus family, my parents looked really great; they're not loud and obnoxious and they don't play stupid practical jokes and they don't invite themselves to dinner at someone else's house. And my dad has *never* called my mom Toots!

Mom came in with the coffee and put a coaster on the table. If we eat in the living room, which we almost never do, she insists we have to use coasters to protect the furniture. Some of it's kind of old, only she calls it antique.

"Ah!" Buck said, taking a swig, "that's mighty good."

If he thought Mom's coffee was good, "Aunt" April must be an awful bad cook. Even Dad admitted that Mom's coffee was barely drinkable. Of course, Buck might have said it just to be polite, but that didn't seem his style.

Rammer was slumped in his chair. He was picking his nose and looked bored.

"This is a lovely home," April said to Mom, as though she hadn't already said it about ten times yesterday.

"We've worked hard on it," Mom answered, and winced when Buck put down his coffee cup *next* to the coaster.

"Say," Buck exclaimed, "aren't there any more of you Martins around? Or have your folks kicked the bucket?"

Dad grit his teeth; I could see the muscles in his jaw tighten. "My mother and father will be here this evening."

"Well, isn't that nice! We'll have an old-fashioned family dinner. Looks like your table is big enough for all of us."

He'd done it again. Mom looked kind of panicked at the idea of cooking them dinner again.

"How long are you staying in Centerville?" Dad asked quickly.

"I have about a week off from my job, so we'll have to mosey back in a couple of days."

Neither Mom nor Dad said anything about how it was too bad they couldn't stay longer. Their tongues would probably have snapped off if they'd bent the truth that far.

Buck winked at Mom. "How about a refill, Toots? And do you have anything sweet to dunk in my cup? A Danish or doughnut — anything you can scrounge up."

Mom smiled, sort of, and walked out. I'd have given my allowance for the next month to have gone with her.

"Say, Nick, old buddy" — this time Buck was looking at me — "I guess you're the next in line. You're a mighty lucky young fellow. It's not everyone who gets to be Santa Claus someday."

"Santa Claus?" I said as stupidly as I could.

Out of the corner of my eye I could see Dad ready to curl up and die. Meanwhile, Marcia looked so angry I think a tornado would have been scared to come her way. How did the new relatives know about the family business?

"Aren't you the next in line?" Buck asked.

"In line for what?"

"To be Santa Claus!"

"Ohhhh!" I exclaimed.

Marcia shot me a warning glance, but I ignored it. I had an idea.

"Santa Claus — of course," I answered in a

soothing tone of voice. "What*ever* you say, Uncle Buck," I finished, sounding like I was talking to a mixed-up two-year-old.

Marcia's face smoothed out, and she bit her lip like she does when she's trying not to laugh. Dad was a little slower catching on, so I hoped he wouldn't say anything.

"What are you talking about?" Buck demanded.

"I wasn't talking about anything," I replied innocently. "You were speaking about" — I stopped and acted like I was choking back a laugh — "that is, you had — Santa Claus on your mind."

Marcia put on a deliberate giggle.

"But aren't you the branch of the family that has charge of the business now?" Buck asked in confusion.

"Not yet," I said, "and to tell you the truth, flowers really aren't my thing. I'm going to be an oceanographer. I'll study the ocean and discover new things and maybe even find out something that will help end pollution."

"Flowers, ocean? What are you talking about?!?" he almost shouted.

"You were talking about the family business — the florist shop," I answered, using that patronizing voice that drives me crazy when people use it on me. "Of course, Fantastic Flowers is pretty

21

nice, and I do make a nice allowance doing deliveries."

"I'm not talking about flowers, I'm talking about Santa Claus, Inc.!"

"Good heavens, Buck," Mom said as she entered the room. "There's no need to shout about it. And you really should know better. After all, it is supposed to be confidential."

I groaned and sank back onto the couch while Buck shot me a look of triumph. Mom had no idea what she'd wrecked.

Buck chuckled. "I knew you were the ones who had the business now. Say, when do I get to meet Santa Claus? Or are you the big guy now?" he asked my dad.

"No." Dad cleared his throat. "My, uh, father is."

"My, my," April giggled. "Part of me never really believed it was true, you know. I thought he was losing his mind when Buck told me the truth the year we were married."

"Yeah!" Rammer said, grinning. "I already got a list you wouldn't believe. No kid'll get more than me next year, since I'll know Santa personally."

"It's more of a delivery business," I warned.

"Hunh?"

"Santa doesn't make presents and hand them out wholesale," Dad explained. "We're mostly a delivery service — kind of like the post office."

Actually, Santa Claus, Inc., is much more than that, and we do give away an awful lot of stuff, but I got the feeling Dad didn't like talking about it with the long-lost relatives.

"You've got to be kidding!" Rammer snorted. "What good is Santa if you can't get what you want from him?"

"Santa Claus is a symbol," Mom tried to say, but Buck and Rammer weren't listening.

"Well, we'll straighten the whole thing out later," Buck interrupted. "For right now, let's go toss the pigskin."

Oh, nooooo! Yesterday's game had been bad enough. Dad and I had bruises all over our arms and legs. Dad sent a look of absolute panic toward Mom.

"Not in my yard again!" Mom proclaimed firmly.

"Of course, dear," Dad told her with a sigh of relief.

"Oh, ho!" Buck chortled, "I guess we know who rules the roost in this family."

Dad just smiled and settled back in his chair.

"Say, Nick" — Buck leaned back and yawned and scratched his stomach — "why don't you tell Rammer here what it's like knowing you'll be Santa Claus someday."

"I won't be."

"You won't be?" Buck sat up in shock. "What do you mean? Aren't you the oldest?"

"Yes, but I'm not going to be Santa. Mar — "

"Why not?" Buck demanded, midsentence.

I sighed. Just thinking of it made me sick to my stomach.

"For one thing, I get airsick in the sleigh."

He stared at me like I was a bug on a plate. "So?"

"And, well, I'm allergic to reindeer."

"Allergic!" he bellowed. "Nonsense! This family has never been allergic to anything."

"Are you sure you're related to us?" I inquired. "Mom says our family by itself probably bought the allergy doctor a sports car."

"That's a lot of hogwash," he answered. "Don't believe in allergies. It's all in the head."

"It certainly is," I answered. "It's in the runny nose and the itchy eyes and the sore throat and the — "

"Hogwash," he said again.

Mom's lips were tight. "Allergies are very real, Buck," she told him through gritted teeth. "We have quite a few on both sides of the family. In fact, I have a feeling I'm getting a new allergy to some, uh, thing right now."

Mom's words didn't phase him a bit; Buck

must have a skin like a rhinoceros. "It's hogwash," he said again. "And even if it wasn't, who'd let a little thing like a runny nose get in the way of being Santa Claus?"

"Me!" I said. "That and getting airsick and because the reindeer don't like me and I'm lousy flying the sleigh and I really want to be an oceanographer."

"Hey!" Rammer said, "if you're not going to be Santa, who is?"

"I am!" Marcia told him.

They all stared at her, their mouths hanging open.

"You're kidding," Buck finally said.

"Nope," Marcia answered. "It all got settled last fall, and I'm Santa after Dad."

"Settled, nothing!" Buck snorted. "Santa's a man's job. Rammer ought to get it!"

CHAPTER 4

"No way!" Marcia shouted. "It's mine! I'm going to be Santa Claus!" At any minute I expected her brown eyes to shoot sparks and smoke to curl out of her ears.

"Don't be a silly, honey. You're a girl."

"Gee, Buck," I said, "thanks for telling us. Marcia, did you know that you're a girl?"

"Right, Nick," Marcia agreed. "Hey, Buck, thanks. I never would have known it, without you."

"A girl can't be Santa."

"Marcia will be the best Santa ever!" Dad suddenly said. It surprised me. He and Granddad hadn't been too happy about giving the job to Marcia, even after they'd agreed to it. But never underestimate the power of an obnoxious new relative butting into our business. Buck and Rammer made Marcia look pretty good.

"We'll see about that!" Buck declared. "We'll just see about that."

Buck, April, and Rammer left right after that but still said they'd be back to eat. So Mom had to rush around getting dinner together for them and for Granddad and Grandma, too, since they were arriving midafternoon.

Marcia stormed up to her room. I followed, with Merry and Christmas behind me. There wasn't much to say, so we just played video games. I got awful hungry, but Marcia was too mad to eat, so I didn't go down to lunch. After all, she is my twin.

Grandma and Granddad got there about two o'clock, and as soon as Marcia heard them at the door, she flew down the stairs.

"They know about Santa Claus, Inc.!" she said.

Granddad frowned. "Well, don't worry, Marcia, if they've kept the secret this long, I suppose they'll keep it up."

"But they want Rammer to be the next Santa!"

"Rammer?"

"He's that monster they call our cousin," I contributed.

Grandma put her arm around Marcia's waist.

"Don't worry," she said, "you're still the next Santa. Isn't that right, dear?" she asked Granddad. He didn't say anything. "Why, Nicholas! I'm surprised at you!" Grandma's voice was stern.

"It's not" — Granddad stopped and scratched his head — "I mean, I'm not sure what to do about this."

"They can't just come in and take the business away, can they?" Marcia demanded.

"It's *your* business, isn't it?" I asked.

"Not quite. It's a family corporation. I've been checking the business charter — in case something came up."

I remember Granddad mentioned it once, a long time ago. He said it had the guidelines for Santa Claus, Inc. But the business always ran like clockwork, so I never looked at it.

"Don't *you* make the decisions?" Marcia asked.

"For most things, but there are rules I have to follow."

I couldn't tell what he was thinking. I know he hadn't wanted Marcia to be Santa. Not that he's against women getting their fair share in the workplace, but he just couldn't picture a girl taking over *Santa Claus*. He eventually gave in, because I stink at it and Marcia is terrific and Grandma insisted and there weren't any other

28

boys in the family to do it anyway. And this Christmas he seemed almost happy about the idea. But now there was a chance that a different boy could take over, and maybe he would change his mind again.

Buck and company arrived about then.

"Hey, Granny," Buck said when he came into the house and saw my grandmother.

Grandma's eyes turned to ice. She doesn't like "Granny," and she hadn't invited Buck to call her anything except Mrs. Martin.

"So, Mr. Claus — "

"Oh, no, Granny," Buck interrupted, "call me Cousin Buck."

He wanted to call Grandma "Granny" but have her call him "cousin"? Buck needed lessons in family structure and genealogy.

"Say, now, where's the big fat guy?" Buck asked.

"That must be me," said Granddad.

Buck's eyes bugged out a little. After all, Granddad is tall, kind of skinny, and he doesn't have a beard. I guess Buck was expecting something, or someone, else.

I couldn't read Granddad's face at all. He shook hands with the new relatives, sat in the living room, chatted about nothing special, and ignored Buck and Rammer's bad manners while he ate dinner. It was after supper that Buck brought up the subject that was sizzling Marcia's temper.

"Now, Gramps, old buddy," Buck said after eating six slices of ham and leaning back to pick his teeth. "Don't you think we ought to discuss Rammer's future in the business?"

"Girls!" Mom interrupted him. "Do you want to go watch television?"

Sandy, Brenda, and Teresa scrambled out of the room as fast as they could. They hadn't enjoyed the grown-up talk, and I don't think they liked the new family members. Sandy had been sitting next to Buck, and it sure wasn't an accident when she dumped a glass of milk on his plate. Afterward she looked around the table with an innocent look and then winked at me. I winked back. Maybe my little sisters aren't *all* bad.

"Buck," Mom told him sternly after the girls were gone, "we never discuss sensitive matters in front of the younger children. They shouldn't be expected to have the discretion of someone older."

He looked blank. Maybe he didn't know what all the words meant. "Oh, well," he said. "How about it? Rammer's here, all eager and waiting to inherit the Santa Claus throne."

Rammer was staring blankly into space.

If he ever became Santa, the world was in trouble.

The big problem was that the family charter wasn't very clear on things like this. It did *not* say that girls couldn't be Santa Claus. It *did* say that the legal heir could name a different successor (I'm the legal heir, so I could name Marcia). But it *also* said that if disagreement arose about it, then another family member had the right to seek the Santa position. After each Santa wanna-be went through apprenticeship training, the whole thing would be settled by a contest on who could do the job best.

When Marcia heard about the contest, she grinned and looked smug. No one could beat her in the sleigh, and she knew it. "I'm willing," she said.

Buck looked at her. "The way I see it, you're not part of this." Buck pointed at me. "*He's* the one who has to compete."

"Me?" I gasped. I got airsick just thinking about it. "No way. Marcia's the one."

"Nope! She's the one you want to take over instead of you. *You're* the heir. If you don't want to be Santa, then Rammer has a right to challenge you for the position."

"That's not what it means, does it, Granddad?" I demanded.

Granddad grimaced. "Unfortunately, Nick, the family charter could be interpreted that way." He turned to my sister. "I'm sorry, Marcia."

I was about to announce that I wouldn't do it — never, no way, no how, no time, no — when I caught sight of two things. One was Marcia. If I said no, then she didn't have a chance. I couldn't let her down, even if she didn't have *much* chance with me competing. The other thing I saw was Buck's face. He was the smug one now. I guess he remembered how bad I was at the Santa stuff and figured that Rammer had it in the bag.

Up until now, I would have said there's nothing I hated worse than flying that sleigh. But now there was definitely something I hated worse, and that was letting Buck and Rammer win!

CHAPTER 5

Summer's the usual time for apprenticeship training. So I thought I'd have until then to prepare my stomach to go flying again. After all, Rammer would need at least five weeks of training before we could compete, and Granddad insisted I'd have to be there, too, for refresher courses. But Buck wasn't willing to wait.

"I want to get my boy's future settled right away," he said. "I don't mind taking him out of school for something important like this, and I can get some extra time from my job."

"Well, I mind taking *Nick* out of school!" Mom answered tartly. But she softened up like a melting marshmallow when she looked at Marcia. Marcia didn't want to wait, either. I knew how she felt. It would be awful hard going through six months of wondering whether she'd get to do what she really wants to do for a career.

So Mom agreed to take me out of school. Well, not exactly. She called my teacher, who gave me six weeks of lessons ahead because we told her my grandparents really needed me to stay with them. Marcia threatened me with death by torture if I didn't give her daily reports on Rammer's progress (she didn't mean it). Mom threatened me with no baseball season if I didn't finish every last school assignment (she really did mean it).

Granddad and Grandma went on ahead, but I had to travel with the relatives. We did the regular route, flying to Norway, then taking the company plane to our own airstrip. The final part of the journey is either by air sleigh or overland. We never fly planes into the North Pole, because they can be detected on radar.

Buck was obnoxious on the commercial flight, always asking the flight attendant for more peanuts or coffee or a pillow or a blanket. She seemed glad to see us leave.

"Sorry, Buck," I said when we were boarding the company plane. "There's no service on this flight. You'll just have to wait on yourself."

"That's okay," he said, and turned to his wife.

"April, why don't you rustle something up for us?" I figured April would put him in his place, but she just jumped up and headed for the front of the plane.

"Hey, April," I called. "You've got to sit down and fasten your seat belt. We're taking off in a couple of minutes."

"Oh, dear," she said, coming back. "Can you wait, honey?" she said with a hopeful look at Buck.

"If it's not too long."

Three seconds after we were level in the air, Buck said, "Okay, Toots, see what you can find."

April trotted forward again.

"She won't find much," I told him. "We don't have service, and we don't stock up on fancy stuff like the airlines."

"Well, that's something we'll change right away." Buck winked at Rammer. "We can't have Santa or his family traveling second class. We'll get a stewardess and all the trimmings."

Buck sure had big plans for the future. And seemed to think that Santa was some sort of royalty. That's never been the company's style. Sure, being Santa Claus is something special. He's loved all over the world. He gets more letters than a movie star. He's the CEO of an international business. But he still cleans up reindeer poop when it hits the ground. We may joke about Santa's throne and castle, but the only crown at the North Pole was on one of Granddad's teeth.

"Here you are, Nick," April said, handing me a cola.

"Thanks, April," I answered. She looked surprised. I'd noticed that Buck doesn't say please or thank you very much. Mom says he got his manners at the zoo.

Rammer wasn't saying much. His face had turned slightly green so I wondered if he was getting airsick. Then he grabbed a couple of candy bars and crammed them down, so I was probably wrong. I don't get sick on the airplane, only on the sleigh. It was just my luck.

For the millionth time I wondered how it turned out this way. Every time I think I've escaped, I get trapped again. Maybe it's some kind of cosmic revenge for turning down Santa Claus.

April's mouth hung open as she stared in disbelief. The sleigh had just arrived to take us to the North Pole.

"What's the matter, Toots?" Buck asked, elbowing April in the side. "Didn't you ever see a sleigh before?"

"It — flew," she managed to say, then turned to me. "I don't think I — believed it, deep down."

I knew what she meant. Even Granddad didn't believe it the time he got amnesia. We told him he was Santa Claus, and he thought we were nuts. So you can't blame April for being surprised. Personally, I think Rammer and Buck were just as amazed, but they were pretending to be cool.

The baggage was loaded in the back.

"Let's get aboard," Granddad said. "It's pretty cold for the reindeer, just standing around."

"I'm not going anywhere in that thing!" April told him.

Buck snorted and then patted her head. "Silly billy."

"Yeah, Mom," Rammer added. "There's nothing to it."

He leaped into the back seat as though he did it every day. But I noticed he took the middle seat and fastened his seat belt first thing.

Buck hustled April onto the seat behind Granddad and then plunked himself into the front seat, which meant I had to sit beside Rammer. We took off, and several things happened at the same time. April shrieked, then leaned forward and grabbed at the closest thing. I don't think she was aiming for Granddad's head, but that's what she got. Granddad's hat went flying, and the sleigh jerked. April shrieked again.

"Stop that!" Granddad yelled. Somehow he managed to safely land the sleigh. But the reindeer were jumping like crazy. "Nick, go grab Donner's harness!"

There wasn't any choice. Buck and Rammer and April were all yelling at each other, and Granddad was working on the antigravity controls for the sleigh. Slowly, I slid out and walked forward. Donner was the lead reindeer.

"Whoa, there, nice reindeer," I said. "Calm down. Nice Donner."

Donner glared. Cautiously I reached for his harness. He snorted and lunged forward. Next thing I knew I was spitting out snow from where I had landed.

"Nice reindeer, my foot," I groaned.

Off in the distance a reindeer wrangler was running toward us. I was tempted to let him handle things, but April was still screaming, and Granddad was yelling at me again to grab Donner's harness.

Somehow I managed to duck in and grab hold of the harness. Donner quieted down, but I didn't trust him. We had a complicated history. I held on even when he snorted some of his bad breath in my direction. Then came the final straw.

"A-a-a-a-choooo!"

Oh, yeah. Allergies were all in the head — my head.

CHAPTER 6

April had hysterics when we tried to go up in the sleigh again. Granddad radioed for snowmobiles, and April insisted Buck and Rammer go with her. I'd rather have gone by snowmobile, too, but then I'd have had to wait in the hangar with them, and I couldn't stand that — even if I had to face the sleigh to get out of it. Five minutes after we were in flight, I grabbed an airsick bag.

"Good grief," Granddad said. "How on earth do you expect to win this competition if you're doing that all the time?"

"Do you want me to win?" I asked through the paper around my mouth.

"You don't think I want that loudmouthed,

puffed-up, lazy idiot and his son to take over?"

"Gee, Granddad, don't hold back, tell me what you really think about them."

He just muttered something into the collar of his coat, so I huddled down and wrapped a blanket around me. It's cold and dark at the North Pole in January, almost twenty-four hours a day. I concentrated on keeping my stomach inside my body.

"After we land," Granddad told me, "go to the house and make sure your grandmother knows that they'll be an extra five hours getting here. She'll have to adjust her dinner plans, and they'll probably want to go straight to bed after they meet everyone."

"You mean they're staying at the house — with *us*?"

"I don't like it, either, but we can't be rude."

"They could have one of the staff apartments."

The North Pole staff has big roomy apartments in an underground complex, and there were always some empty ones. Granddad treats his employees really well. No dorms. They have a gym, a pool, and a heated conservatory with lots of plants and flowers and even vegetables. I didn't think it was so awful to put Buck and company over there.

"It wouldn't be right," Granddad said.

"Then can *I* stay in one of the staff apartments?"

"If I have to put up with them, *so do you!*"

I guess that was only fair.

The division supervisors were all waiting for us when we arrived. Granddad said it was supposed to be an official delegation. Granddad might not like the new relatives, but he was determined to follow proper protocol.

"Sorry, folks," he called. "Our visitors are coming overland."

Everyone else left, except Randolph. Randolph is head of the office staff. Randolph and I don't get along. Last year when I tried to computerize the office, he convinced the other workers to strike. And then, just a few days ago, he was supposed to fly with me on the Santa Claus rounds, but he got the stomach flu instead and had to recover in a motel. He looked kind of sheepish, like he didn't know how to act around me. So I decided to set things straight and let Randolph know that nothing had changed between us.

"Hi, Rudolph! How's the nose?" Yes, his name is really Randolph, but I'm always mixing the name up anyway, and he hates it.

The embarrassed expression left his face, and he glared at me, which made us both more comfortable. I don't know how I'd handle it if Randolph felt like he actually had to be my friend.

"You need me for anything, Mr. Martin?" he asked Granddad.

"Yes. Please let the entire staff know we'll have a meeting tonight at eight."

"Right." He tipped his hat at Granddad, growled something at me I couldn't understand, and then stomped off to the main building. I guess I should have tried to get him on my side, but I didn't think he was going to cheer for Rammer anyway.

"Where're the elves?" Rammer demanded when the Clauses finally arrived at the North Pole and all they saw were regular people.

"There aren't any," I told him. "Just short Laplanders, and a few tall ones. Santa Claus is an equal opportunity employer."

Rammer shrugged, but his father frowned.

"There's gotta be elves," Buck told me.

"We aren't hiding any in the basement. Trust me, Buck. There *aren't* any elves."

"Can't we get some?"

"And where do you suggest we find them? Elves R Us?"

He stared at me like he thought I had elves

hidden in my hip pocket. "I thought Santa Claus had elves."

I guess the family stories had gotten mixed up with fairy tales, and he didn't know which were which. Which gave me an idea.

"Actually" — I leaned forward to whisper — "I guess I should tell you the truth, since you're family and all. We do have elves, only some of them are a little tall. They're a bit embarrassed about the whole thing and would rather pretend that they're human. The head elf is Randolph, in the office. You can't miss him — he's got the reddest nose in the place. He can tell you who the other elves are, if he wants. Sometimes he pretends he doesn't know anything about it, but he knows, so just keep asking. I think they've got some really short elves stashed away somewhere, but they're kind of shy. Maybe you can do something about that — you know, help them feel more comfortable being around us . . . big people."

Buck winked.

If there's anything Randolph likes less than he likes me, it's being asked about elves.

"Uh, hem." Granddad cleared his throat for about the fifth time. "I'd like to — introduce you to some long-lost members of the family. This is the Claus family, Buck, April, and, er, Rammer."

There was polite applause. Some of the reindeer wranglers were trying hard not to smile. They'd seen April and Buck's scene at the airstrip.

"We've, uh, come to an unusual situation here. Rammer has challenged Nick for the right to become Santa Claus someday. After his apprenticeship training, a contest will be held to see who is the more qualified."

There was dead silence. I'd thought Granddad would mention Marcia, but then he just told everyone good night. As we were leaving, the office people were talking.

"That was some bombshell he dropped," one man said.

"Well, if it's going to be *him* and not his sister, I'm rooting for that Rammer kid."

He turned red when he realized I'd heard him, but I didn't hold it against him. If it weren't for Marcia and Rammer and the fact that Buck is totally obnoxious, I'd have been rooting for Rammer, too.

CHAPTER

★ 7 ★

Rammer started training the day after we arrived (the next day by the clock, since the sun didn't rise and set). I was tired. My room was next to Buck's, and it turned out that he snores. Loud. Really loud. I'm surprised he doesn't show up on seismic readings. During the brief periods I did get to sleep, I dreamed of swooping around in the sleigh and getting sick to my stomach while a snorting monster came racing after me. Then Buck would give an especially loud snore, and I'd wake up dizzy.

"I hope you slept well," Grandma said to Buck at breakfast.

"Like a log," he answered. "Nothing ever bothers me."

I could believe that.

After breakfast, Buck insisted everyone gather outside for Rammer's first takeoff, like it was an Olympic event.

"This is a moment to remember," he announced. "The first step to becoming Santa Claus."

"Only if he wins the contest," Grandma said sharply.

"Of course, Granny," Buck told her in a patronizing voice. Grandma's eyes snapped like firecrackers, but all she did was stomp back into the house. "Hey, you're going to miss it!" Buck called, but Grandma ignored him.

While that was happening, April was staring at the sleigh like she'd seen a monster herself. "You aren't letting him fly that thing, are you?" she finally demanded.

"He won't solo for a couple of weeks," Granddad explained.

"Solo?"

"Now, Toots," Buck said, "don't interfere. This is men's business. Rammer's got to fly the sleigh to win the contest."

Granddad and Rammer took off. April went back inside to huddle beside the fireplace. I disappeared into my room.

Those first few days weren't very promising — for Marcia.

If life were fair, I would have discovered an amazing ability to fly the sleigh when I got back to the North Pole, and Rammer would have been awful at it. Or at least he would have been worse than I am.

Life isn't fair. Rammer turned out to be a fairly decent pilot. Not as good as Marcia, but after only a few lessons he looked much better than I did. I'm not sure the reindeer liked him, but they didn't hate him, either.

I expected to ace Rammer on the written test — you know, the flight routes, world Christmas customs, stuff like that. Rammer turned out to be good in the stuff that needed math but not much good in anything else. The problem is that the written part isn't that important, since someone could always help Santa with those things. But only Santa flies the sleigh on Christmas Eve and delivers the toys (unless he has the flu). The written test would only count if Rammer and I were equal on the sleigh. Marcia got more and more upset every time I called her.

Since I'd already had my apprenticeship training, Granddad worked with Rammer every day. But on the fourth morning, I screwed up my stomach and prepared to go into the air.

"Nice boy," I said to Donner when I was ready to hitch him up in the barn. He gave me the evil eye, or at least that's what I'd call it. I sneezed and dropped the harness.

Rammer and Buck had come out to watch. "Say, that reindeer don't seem to like you much," Buck said.

"I'm Donner's favorite person in the whole world," I said rashly, and bent over to retrieve the harness. That's when I saw it — out of the corner of my eye. Donner's foot was aimed right at my backside. I dove to get away from him and landed on a pile of straw.

The straw wasn't clean.

Rammer snorted. "Didn't know you liked manure so much. Yeah, that reindeer just plain loves you."

Ignoring him, I finished getting the sleigh ready, then stomped into the back room to change my clothing. There was no way I was going flying with that stuff on my jacket. I'd have enough trouble keeping my breakfast down.

One of the reindeer wranglers had the double doors open by the time I got back. Granddad came in while I was climbing aboard. "Just hold them steady, with a firm hand, Nick."

"Sure, Granddad. Just like always." I was lying through my teeth.

"Giddyup!" I said, as steady and firm as I could manage. They just stood there, so I slapped the reins while Rammer snickered and said loudly, "Giddyup!!!"

The reindeer started. The sleigh started. The reindeer lifted off, but the sleigh didn't. Somehow the harness had broken loose. I couldn't believe it. I'd hitched it up myself, and I *knew* I'd done it right.

"Nick!" Granddad roared. "Can't you even harness that sleigh properly?" He whistled loud, and the reindeer turned back and landed. "Well?" he demanded. When I didn't say anything, he threw his hands into the air and stomped off.

Buck was laughing so hard he fell into the snow. "They'll do anything to get away from you, won't they, Nick?" he snickered, and I suddenly knew what must have happened.

"Very funny, Buck," I said with a sneer.

"Don't get your intestines in a knot. You weren't in any danger."

I didn't answer, just rehitched the sleigh and wobbled into the air. I think I was getting worse at flying. I'd be lucky if Marcia would ever forgive me.

The next day Marcia arrived at the North Pole. Mom said she was in such a bad mood, she might as well be grouchy around the new relatives instead of at home.

"Hi, Toots!" I said when she got out of the snowmobile.

"Not funny," she grumbled.

I was really glad to see her. Now I'd have someone to watch my back — and my seat. Every time I turned around, Buck or Rammer put a pile of reindeer poop on my chair. Marcia and I could watch out for each other.

But it also meant more flight time. She could coach me on the backup sleigh and team.

"I've been thinking," Marcia said.

"Congratulations," I mumbled. I wasn't very happy. Marcia hadn't even gone to the house yet because she dragged me straight to the barn for a practice flight.

"You've got to do a Möbius," Marcia told me.

"A Möbius!!!" I practically screeched. "No way!"

A Möbius is hard to explain. Take a strip of paper, and bring it together like you were going to make a link for a paper chain. But instead of pasting the ends so it makes a smooth loop, twist one end upside down and then glue it to the other end. It makes a loop with a half twist in it, and it's like the paper only has one side. You can draw a line lengthwise along that paper loop, and it will meet itself. The line will be on both sides of the paper, and you don't even have to lift the pen.

I know it sounds impossible. But if you think it's tricky with paper, try doing it in the sleigh. You go upside down and on a corkscrew. The loops do awful things to my stomach. Marcia can do it without half trying, but Granddad's been trying for years to get it right. There was no way *I'd* be able to ever do one, and I don't want to: it's *dangerous*.

"You've got to, Nicky," Marcia told me. "If you can do a really fancy maneuver like that, then you'll win for sure."

My head swam in circles just thinking about it. Then I saw the pile of reindeer droppings on the seat of the sleigh.

"Okay, I'll try. But you clean up the poop this time."

"Now, just glide into it and dip the reins down and to the left," Marcia said. "Do a pretty big Möbius until you get the hang of it, then we'll get smaller."

"But we'll be upside down for longer."

"It's okay. We've got the seat belts now."

That wasn't exactly reassuring, but I carefully wobbled the sleigh into position and did just what she said. For a minute I thought I'd got it. We slid through the first part of the loop, and we went upside down. (Even with the seat belt I had my feet braced under the foot bars.) It didn't do a thing for my stomach. I quickly pulled for the upside part of the loop, and nothing happened. I pulled again, then jerked, but the reindeer seemed perfectly happy flying along upside down.

"This isn't it, Nicky," Marcia told me.

"No kidding," I hissed, and shoved the reins into her hands. "Get this thing turned around!"

The reindeer could tell it wasn't me flying anymore, and when Marcia twitched on the reins they did exactly what they were supposed to do. "Try it again, Nick," she insisted when we were upright again.

"In a minute," I mumbled into my paper bag. "In a minute."

CHAPTER

8

"I've decided the two of you will come with me on the January sixth gift flight," Granddad announced that night at dinner.

"Hunh?" Rammer mumbled, his mouth crammed full of Grandma's pot roast.

"It's a shorter delivery list, and it'll work out quite well. I can observe the two of you in action."

"But aren't you through for the year?" April asked nervously.

"Christmas is celebrated at different times in some cultures, but many of them still want Santa to come. Some of the cultures call me things other than Santa, like Grandfather Frost or Father Christmas. Most of the deliveries on January sixth will be in Russia and a few other places where Russians live and keep the old customs."

"Oh." April didn't look happy about the trip.

"Can I go, too?" Marcia demanded. "I really want to see what the Santa deliveries are like in case I . . ." Her voice trailed off. I don't think she wanted to say it out loud in case she didn't get to be Santa after the contest.

"Okay, Marcia." Granddad's voice was kind of gruff. Then he shook his head and said, "Well, this has been a wonderful supper. Nick, tonight let's you and me get the table cleared and the dishes washed before we have dessert."

"Oh, let me help," April said, like she always did.

"Nope," Granddad told her. "That's our job." He cleaned the kitchen every night, and Buck had mostly stopped laughing about it, at least when Granddad was around.

Cleanup didn't take long. The kitchen has all the modern gadgets and a few others that my ancestor (the one who figured out how to make the sleigh fly) had invented that the world hadn't gotten around to thinking of yet. It got me wondering about him. The next day Marcia was still asleep, trying to catch up to the different time zone, and Rammer was doing flight practice with Granddad. So I decided to explore my genius ancestor's workshop. April came by while I was examining a piece of equipment.

"Oh," I said, "how are you this morning?"

She shrugged nervously. "I decided to take a little walk, but it's so cold and dark. I saw the light. Is it all right if I come in here with you?"

"No problem."

I didn't mind April as much as Buck and Rammer, especially if they weren't with her.

"What's that?" She pointed at the weird contraption I'd been poking at.

"I haven't the slightest idea. This was my great-great-great-great-grandfather's workshop. At least, I think that's how many greats it was. He's the one who came up with the antigrav sleigh and the subatomic radiophone and all kinds of other gadgets that make Santa Claus work so well. Pretty amazing, considering it was a long time before Orville and Wilbur Wright ever got off the ground at Kitty Hawk."

"That's wonderful. But isn't it kind of dusty in here?" she said. Picking up a rag, she started polishing the thingamajig.

"No one comes in here much."

"Hmmmm," she murmured when she saw the drawings lying next to it. "It looks like he hadn't finished putting this one together."

"Yeah, well, from what I've heard, he was

working on stuff right up till the day he died."

"I wonder if this is unfinished because he didn't have enough time or because he decided it wouldn't work?"

I shrugged. "Search me."

There were several parts on the counter. "This should fit right here," she said, and fitted it into place. She studied the drawing again. "And this one screws on after it."

She was right, they did fit, and after a few more parts, the gadget slowly started looking more like the drawing.

"You're really good at this," I told April.

"Oh." She stopped and looked embarrassed. "Not really. I'm sure you're much better."

"Not a chance. I didn't even realize that was the right drawing." She looked pleased. "Are you some kind of engineer?" I asked.

"Oh, no. I'm a bookkeeper for several businesses."

Now I knew where Rammer got his math skills. It sure wasn't from Buck.

"You must do a pretty good business as an accountant," I said.

"Well, I don't take very many clients. I just keep a desk at the house since Buck doesn't like me going out to work."

Marcia kept telling me that Buck was a cave-

man in disguise. Of course, she was already prejudiced against him, but she might still be right.

"You know," April said, turning back to the machine she'd been working on, "I can't really tell
what this gadget is for, except — you'll think I'm
silly."

"No way."

"Well, if I didn't know better, I'd say it was a
time machine, but some of the parts are missing."

I didn't say anything. It did sound a little crazy,
but most of great-great-great-great-grandfather's
gadgets would *still* seem impossible to most
people. Maybe he *had* invented a time machine
and just hadn't finished it. Which was too bad.
Maybe then I could go back to that day Buck
first rang the doorbell and I wouldn't answer it.
Or maybe I could tell him that the Martins had
just moved to Timbuktu and weren't expected
back for thirty or forty years. Yeah, that would
work. Too bad the machine didn't.

"I want a word with you!" Randolph roared.

I'd walked into the office building looking for
Marcia and hadn't thought about meeting up
with Randolph.

"Uhhhh, yes?" I answered.

"Did you tell Buck Claus that I was an elf?"

I smiled innocently. "Well, he was totally convinced there were elves hiding around here. So I said that he should ask you about them."

His face turned red. "And?!?"

"And I probably did say you were an elf, you know, to get him off my case."

His face turned purple, except for his nose; it stayed red. I saw Marcia peeking around the corner. She grinned and waved at me.

I smiled and turned my head and narrowed my eyes. "You know what? When I look at you from just the right angle, your ears do look like they've got points on them. Are you *sure* that you aren't an elf?"

"Argggggggggh!" he yelled, and stomped off.

Marcia stepped out of hiding. She was laughing so hard she couldn't stand straight.

"You missed the part where Buck was talking to him," she told me. "Buck kept patting him on the shoulder and saying he knew the truth and there was no need to be ashamed of being an elf. Randolph nearly exploded."

I raised my hands in a victory sign. It's not every day you can score one off both Randolph *and* an obnoxious relative.

CHAPTER 2

I had thought that the last time I'd stepped out of the sleigh would be the last time, *ever*. I mean, it had been the first time Santa had ever gotten sick on Christmas Eve, so I was safe, right? No one would need a substitute Santa for another thousand years. But now I was getting ready to spend another night in the sleigh.

I stocked up on airsick bags and tried to think positive.

Marcia was thrilled about the coming flight, but Rammer acted like he didn't care one way or the other.

"Aren't you supposed to be dressed like a little old lady?" Rammer asked Granddad.

"What do you mean?" I asked, since Granddad

wasn't listening. He had on his special Grandfather Frost suit. It was a creamy white with a long, robelike coat. It wasn't as convenient to wear as his regular Santa Claus suit, but Granddad says that's what Grandfather Frost should wear.

Rammer snapped his gum and said, "You know, like that baboon lady in Russia."

"I don't know what you're talking about." I really had no idea.

"And you think you're so smart and know that stuff. I'll beat you on the written test for sure."

Marcia and I stared at each other and shrugged. The written test? Baboon lady? He was a bit nuts, if you ask me. I thought that *he* might be a baboon from — but then I realized he probably meant the old lady who brings gifts to kids in Russia. The story says she had a chance to join the Wise Men on their journey, but she passed it up to clean her house and has been sorry ever since. But because she likes kids, she brings them presents for Christmas.

"Do you mean Babouschka?" I asked.

"Yeah. The baboon lady."

"Right, Rammer," I humored him, "you're going to ace the written test."

"Well, who cares about people stupid enough to believe stuff like that anyway?"

Granddad heard that part and was glaring like crazy. Rammer had just broken one of the company's top rules about respecting other cultures and their Christmas customs.

"Get aboard," Granddad roared, "and change your attitude!"

Rammer just shrugged and climbed into the sleigh. Marcia had put a big bag of stuff there so she had to move it before he could sit down.

Rammer screeched. "Yikes! Why don't you have seat warmers in this thing?"

"We do," Marcia said innocently, and tossed her bag of stuff into an empty compartment. She settled back with a grin, and I knew why. She'd sneaked a whole package of dry ice out of the storage barn. Even the seat warmers couldn't keep up with that.

Russia went off without a hitch. I think Rammer was a little nervous, because I heard him muttering something about the secret police and Siberia. Maybe he hadn't heard that Russia has gone democratic.

Not that I was paying all that much attention. Between getting airsick and being dizzy from the M*E*D*A*R (the Matter Energy Disassemble and Reassemble device we use to get in and out of houses without going down the chimneys), I didn't feel so good. Of course, I already knew how to use the M*E*D*A*R device, since I'd done the Santa rounds on Christmas Eve. But Marcia hadn't had a chance. And since the whole point was to see how well I did it, Granddad wouldn't let Marcia go into houses unless she was going with me.

Some of the time Granddad went with Rammer, to show him the ropes. Part of the time, Rammer went alone. That turned out to be a big mistake. Rammer brought his superglue with him and glued three Christmas trees and seven sets of shoes to the floor. Granddad's complaint department worked for three months to clear up the mess.

It was my turn at the first house we hit in the United States. Marcia and I M*E*D*A*Red in and started to work.

"I'll get the stockings, you do the Christmas tree," I suggested.

"It's a yolka," Marcia said.

I'd forgotten that's what the Russians call their Christmas trees. "Okay," I agreed, "you put the packages around the yolka."

"Yolka, yolka, which egg lost its yolka," a voice chanted. I swiveled around and found Rammer grinning from the corner.

"What are you doing here?"

"You missed a package." He held it up. I remembered putting it in, so he must have sneaked it out of the bag.

He handed it to Marcia and waited. Then I saw the mouse clinging to the ribbons. Rammer started to laugh. "Eeek, eeek!" he said.

"Nice try, but you're out of luck, Rammer," I told him. "My sister isn't scared of mice."

Marcia just plucked the mouse off the package and handed it back to him. He shrugged, then punched his M*E*D*A*R button and disappeared. Three seconds later the mouse appeared where he'd been standing; he must have sent it back in.

"We've got to catch it!" I whispered.

The mouse just kind of stood there like it was dazed; it isn't every day a mouse gets its cells rearranged, sent through a roof, and then put back together. I started to tiptoe in its direction. For a minute I thought it would stay there and wait for me, but then it caught sight of an enemy. Not me. A cat.

The cat was half asleep, but the mouse wasn't taking any chances. It scurried toward the Christmas tree. I lunged for it and belly flopped on the floor.

"Careful!" Marcia hissed. "You'll wake everyone up!"

Like I didn't already know that. I crawled under the Christmas tree. A piece of tinsel got tangled around my ear, and I was about to pull it off when something whacked against the side of my face. I turned my head and saw the cat. Did I say cat? It was bigger than any house cat *I* had ever seen, and it had sharp white teeth and claws. It swiped at the tinsel again, and I ducked to save my skin. Then the mouse scooted past me under a pile of packages. The cat let out a screech and started scratching at the pile like it was drilling for oil. Bits of wrapping paper went flying. I grabbed for the mouse just in time and nearly lost a hand doing it. Somehow I managed to hand the mouse to Marcia, then stared at the mess.

"What'll we do?" Marcia demanded.

"Leave it!" I told her. "The cat'll get the blame, not us."

"But it's our fault, sort of, and we're supposed to leave everything in perfect order."

"Forget it, Marcia," I groaned as I pulled myself out from under the tree. "You wanted to know what the real Santa deliveries are like? This is it. Sometimes it's Mess City."

"But Rammer started this."

"And if he didn't, something else would have. Think about it, Sis." I dabbed at the bloody scratches on my hand. "It isn't always like the storybooks make it sound. Say the word, and Rammer gets the job."

"Are you nuts?" she asked. "This is even more fun than I thought it would be."

She thought this was *fun?* One of us had to be nuts, and now I was pretty sure it was her.

CHAPTER 10

"What happened, and what took so long?" Granddad growled when we got back to the roof.

"Reality," I told him. "With a little Rammer mixed in." I plopped down on the seat and shot right back up again. It was *freezing*! I saw Rammer shoving Marcia's package of dry ice under the seat.

"Would you like something to sit on?" he asked, holding up his whoopee cushion.

"Sure!" I grabbed it, sat down, and ignored the disgusting sound it made. I fastened my seat belt, leaned back, and closed my eyes.

Rammer's mouth opened like a fish. "Hey! Give it back!"

I yawned in his face. "You offered it to me."

"But I — "

"I heard you," Marcia said innocently.

"So did I," Granddad added, with a straight face.

I hung on to the cushion until after Rammer came out from the next house. Or I should say I put it back on his seat and leaned back with my eyes closed like I hadn't moved a muscle. He didn't bother looking and ended up sitting on his own whoopee cushion. You know, sometimes things go the way they should.

And sometimes they don't.

At the next stop, Granddad said he'd go in with Marcia and me. "I've got to see how you're doing," he explained, but I think he just wanted to get away from Rammer. Everything went the way it's supposed to, and we M*E*D*A*Red back to the roof. Only it *wasn't* the roof of the *house*; we were standing on the top of a *gas station*!

The sleigh was on the roof, but Rammer was gone.

"That — that — " Granddad spluttered. "He's not ready for solo flying!"

"Take it easy," Marcia told him.

I was dizzy from the trip, so it took me a minute to figure out what had happened. Rammer must have taken off and flown down the block to the gas station. If he'd gone much farther, we'd have been stuck at that last house, since M*E*D*A*R has limited range. We were kind of hidden behind a sign, so maybe no one would see us from the ground.

Marcia said, "Don't worry, Granddad, we'll go find him." She trotted to the side of the flat roof and started down the ladder. Before she disappeared, she waved at me to follow.

I gingerly stepped to the ladder; she was already at the bottom. She had to be kidding. Going down thirty-foot ladders isn't my thing. Instead I hit my M*E*D*A*R button and arrived at ground level the safe, sensible way.

"You shouldn't have done that. You can't just use M*E*D*A*R whenever you want," Marcia scolded. "What if someone saw you?"

"I looked first."

"That's what the mouse said just before the cat swallowed him."

"Do you want to complain or look for Rammer?"

"Come on."

We trotted around to the front of the station where they had one of those convenience stores. Rammer was inside, cramming down a corn dog. Rammer eats more than anyone I ever saw before.

"Hi, guys," he mumbled around a mouthful. "You finished already?"

"Yessss!" Marcia hissed. "And what do you think you're doing?"

"Just thought I'd get a snack," he said, and licked some mustard off his sleeve.

"Hey! What are you kids doing out so late?" a gruff voice asked. It was a stern-looking man in some kind of security uniform. I gulped.

"We're, uh, here with our grandfather," Rammer answered. He'd turned pale.

"Which one is he?"

Rammer pointed at an old guy who'd just finished filling his tank. He should have picked someone else, because just then the man climbed behind his wheel and drove away.

"Your grandfather just left," the man said.

"He's, uh, kind of senile," Rammer told him. "After a few minutes Gramps'll remember and come back for us."

Rammer sounded smoother than he looked. From what I could see, he was ready to crack like an egg.

"In case he doesn't remember," the man said, "I think I'd better call and have the police pick you up. We can't have youngsters running around this late by themselves."

Rammer's nerves turned to panic. "No, sir!" he yelled. "I'll tell the truth. He's on the roof in Santa's sleigh. Check and see for yourself!"

What?! If he did that, then we were sunk!

Granddad says that Santa Claus is supposed to be one of those things you only see at the corner of your eye and feel at the tips of your imagination. North Pole security is always careful to protect that and to keep my ancestor's inventions a secret. When Granddad was missing, Marcia and I got caught once, but I passed it off as a publicity stunt. That wasn't going to work with this guy, and I knew it.

"You're either nuts or the biggest liar I ever saw," the man told Rammer. "But either way, it doesn't matter. I'm calling the police. I think we've got a curfew in this town."

I could see Rammer jabbing at his M*E*D*A*R button, and I grabbed his arm. If he just disappeared we'd be sunk.

My brain finally clicked into gear. "Wait, please!" I said, then turned to Marcia. "Why don't you take our poor cousin out for some fresh air on the way home. Isn't that what the therapist said we should do when he gets like this?"

Marcia's no dummy. She probably couldn't guess what I was up to but was smart enough to play along.

"Yes, of course, Nick," she said sweetly. "Poor Rammer, don't worry, we'll take care of you."

"What's the big idea?" Rammer demanded, but Marcia grabbed his arm and hustled him out before he could say anything else.

"I'm so sorry," I told the security guy. "But my cousin gets like this sometimes. You're right about the lying." I shook my head sadly. "He's been doing that ever since he was three years old and he tried to knock over a tree with his head. That's why we call him Rammer."

The man nodded sympathetically, and I could tell I had him hooked.

"He sees a psychiatrist three times a week, and we've got him down to maybe three lies a day, but sometimes he just sort of relapses." I let my shoulders sag. "It's going to be awful explaining how he sneaked out tonight. We live just a few houses down, and Marcia and I wanted to get him back before anyone found out."

"Okay, but you'd better hurry home. It's too late for kids your age to be out, especially considering Rammer's condition."

I trotted around the corner of the building where he couldn't see me. With the M*E*D*A*R, I got to the sleigh in about two seconds. Marcia and Rammer were already there.

"Let's get out of here!" Granddad said.

CHAPTER

11

For a week almost every other word Granddad said to Rammer had something to do with the fiasco at the service station.

"Gee, he's sure a drip about it," Rammer complained. "When do you think he'll dry up?"

"Maybe never," I told him, and couldn't resist rubbing it in. "I mean, if you want to be Santa Claus, you've got to know how to do it right, and that's definitely not how *you* did it."

He just made a face.

The next day, Rammer and Granddad went off for a flight lesson. Rammer didn't think he needed it. "After all," he told me, "I managed a perfect solo flight to the gas station."

I nearly choked on my bacon. "I wouldn't mention that, if I were you."

Marcia and I were waiting when they got back, since Marcia wanted me to practice with the lead reindeer team. Rammer managed a perfect landing, and Marcia's shoulders slumped. "The reindeer even like him!" she hissed.

"They like you, too," I said. "As Grandma says, there's no accounting for taste."

"Ha-ha."

Rammer hopped down from the sleigh and stood watching as Granddad reset the antigrav controls and stood up.

Rrrrrrriiiiipppp!

"What the —!" Granddad roared and looked behind him. A huge piece of his pants was lying on the seat. He frowned and tugged at the fabric; it didn't budge.

Rammer started snorting. "How about a little air-conditioning?" he managed to choke out.

It was another one of Rammer's stupid practical jokes. He must have smeared glue all over Granddad's section of the sleigh.

"It's below freezing. I don't need air-conditioning. I'll deal with you later!" Granddad growled at Rammer. He marched away with as much dignity as he could, but even the reindeer wranglers were stuffing straw in their mouths to keep from laughing. I didn't laugh. After all, I lost the seat of my pants, too, when I flew the sleigh last Christmas. But at least I was wearing jeans underneath, not snowflake-patterned long johns.

You'd think that Rammer would have enough sense not to get Granddad riled up; after all, he's the one who will finally decide the contest. Even Buck wasn't happy when he found out about the glue. I accidentally overheard their father-son conversation. Okay, so it wasn't by accident.

"That was really stupid," Buck growled at Rammer.

"It was funny. Lots of people laughed."

"Don't do it again! We need Gramps on our side."

I told Marcia about it when we finally headed out on our flight. "It won't make any difference," Marcia said with a gloomy face. "Granddad's so fair, he won't count Rammer down, even for that. So you've got to get the Möbius, Nicky!"

We tried another Möbius and ended flying upside down without turning right side up when we were supposed to again.

"I hope you didn't tell Granddad I was going to do one of those things," I mumbled.

"No." She sighed and got us upright. "I wanted you to surprise him, but I guess you'd better not bring it up."

I mumbled, "Too late," and grabbed for a spare airsick bag.

Rammer got better at flying during the next few weeks. I got worse, if it's possible to go down from zero. When I could escape from Marcia's drilling, I spent time in great-great-great-great-granddad's shop. April sometimes came, too, and I actually started to like hanging out with her.

"How can you?" Marcia demanded.

"What's the problem?" I asked. "It's not helping Rammer."

"It's like — consorting with the enemy."

"Nah, April's okay, as long as Buck isn't around. She's actually kind of smart, and funny, too."

Marcia's mouth dropped open. "Are we talking about the same person?"

It wasn't Marcia's fault; she'd never spent time with April by herself. Besides, she was prejudiced against anyone connected with Rammer. But April wasn't bad company. I wouldn't have minded having her for an aunt, if only Buck didn't come with the deal.

That afternoon April and I worked on a little gadget that great-great-great-great-granddad must have had a use for, but we didn't know what it was.

"I think it's a miniature furnace," April finally said.

Sure enough, when she flipped a switch, it put out a nice, warm breeze.

"You're pretty smart," I told her.

"Thanks," she said, beaming.

Maybe I shouldn't have opened my big mouth again, but sometimes it has a life of its own. There was something I just had to say, but I wasn't sure how to start. "April, Buck sure — uh — seems to boss you around a lot."

"Well . . ." She smiled weakly. "He doesn't really mean it. He has old-fashioned ideas."

"Well, I don't see why he can't get his own coffee. He can't expect you to do everything. Maybe you should tell him so."

Her eyes opened wide. "Oh, dear. I couldn't do that!"

"Why not?"

"I . . ." She stopped and frowned. She left after that, shaking her head. I was pretty sure she was mad at me. It wasn't until later that I found out what I'd started.

"Hey, April, how about you get me a cup of coffee and some goodies," Buck said from where he was comfortably sprawled in front of the family room fire.

April leaned back and thumbed through her magazine.

"Didn't you hear me, Toots?" Buck said a little louder.

"Certainly, Buck," she answered, and picked up another magazine.

"Well, how about it?"

"How about what, dear?"

"My coffee!" Buck almost yelled. His face was turning bright red.

"Oh, yes. There *is* a pot in the kitchen if you want some."

My eyes nearly bulged out of their sockets. April put her feet up on a footstool, yawned, and picked up another magazine.

"What!" Buck did yell this time.

"Yes, dear?" April looked up. "And if you're getting a cup for yourself, would you mind getting some for me?"

"Mom?" Rammer said, his eyes bulging even more than mine.

"What is it, Steve?"

He blinked, and I wondered if he even remembered that Steve was his real name, and not Rammer.

"Are you okay?" he asked after a minute.

April stretched. "Perfectly all right. In fact, I feel just great. Why?"

"Oh. I just wondered." He looked at Buck, whose face was turning purple by now. Then he jumped to his feet. "I'll get your coffee, Dad."

"Don't be silly, Steve." April shook her head at him. "You've worked hard all day, and your father is perfectly able to pour his own coffee. He knows how, I think."

Buck looked like a ten-ton truck had hit him. Maybe it had. Rammer was staring at his mother like she'd been possessed by aliens and would sprout some weird antennae any minute.

"Sit down, Steve," April said. She ignored Buck, who finally stomped off toward the kitchen. "Tell me how the lessons are going."

"J-Just fine, Mom."

"Do you enjoy it? You know you don't have to do it, if you don't like it."

"Uh, yeah, I guess it's okay."

It was a really strange evening.

CHAPTER
12

The next day was the big one. Contest time.

When Buck or Rammer was around, Marcia acted cocky and confident. "Nick has got you beat in the first ten inches," she proclaimed to Rammer.

He just grinned and acted superior, as usual. The only crack came whenever he looked at his mother.

It was the morning after April's initial revolt. She came downstairs without her curls, coolly walked past Buck, got herself a cup of coffee, and sat down.

Rammer looked up and gave her a smile. Buck looked disappointed, like he'd hoped the night before had been just a bad dream. "April, how about a — " he started to say when she glanced at him with an eyebrow raised. "I mean, uh, would you like cream with your coffee?"

As revolutions go, this wasn't bad. It looked like April had won the big battle.

Like I'd expected, I aced the written test. Rammer did really well on the part that needed math, like speed, distance, and arrival times. But I left him in the dust over Christmas customs, history, routes, and general business practice. Granddad gave the written test first, which was good, since my brain might not have worked so well after flying the sleigh.

The flying part of the contest was set up to include several things: skill in holding the sleigh steady, ability to land on a small space like a roof, maneuverability in tight spaces when you have to fly low, technique in managing the antigrav and other high-tech gadgets, control over the reindeer team (I was in big trouble on that one). Speed wasn't important, that was just mechanics.

Of course, there's a lot more to being Santa Claus than flying. Santa is the head of a huge business with hundreds of employees. But there wasn't any contest event that could prove which person could handle that part. Buck suggested that the employees vote, but Granddad said it wouldn't be fair, since I was his grandson and they might vote for me out of loyalty. (He may have been wrong about that; the staff once went out on strike because of me. If Marcia was competing, it'd be a different story.)

"In any case," Granddad told Buck, "this isn't a popularity contest."

Too bad we couldn't get some outsiders to vote — I might have won. Not because I'm so terrific, but would you want a Santa who might glue your pants to the chair?

My stomach started churning as soon as we headed for the barn. Granddad said that, to be fair, we each had to go on the other's flight. Buck invited himself along, so I said Marcia should come, too. Marcia was already depressed but was hiding it pretty well.

We were tossing a coin to see who'd go first.

"Here goes," Granddad said as the coin flew into the air. "Heads means Nick is first. Tails is Rammer."

He was using an American quarter, and I held my breath to see if I got Washington's head. I did! At least I wouldn't be airsick starting out, like I would if Rammer was first. I climbed into the sleigh, picked up the reins with as much authority as I could manage, and we were off.

"Good takeoff," Granddad told me.

Granddad wasn't just being nice; it probably *was* the best I'd ever done. I even managed to keep the reindeer stable as I landed and took off for several pretend "roof landings." They went fine!

Then we started on the long part of the run, to show altitude control and general flying ability. This is where it would have been great to do the Möbius, but the way things were going, maybe I'd be all right without it. No way would I mess with the best flight of my life! As we came closer to the place where Marcia and I had practiced the fancy maneuver, I turned around to grin at her.

"Guess I don't need to bring it up, after all," I told her.

"Bring what up?" Buck demanded.

I turned to the front and grinned again when I heard Marcia tell him, "Nothing, just something Nick has got in the bag."

A feeling of triumph started creeping over me. I should have known better; that's when disaster usually strikes.

We were almost to the halfway point, and I

calculated how far I had to go before turning back. The turn would be a simple move, and then there was only the return to the landing strip and the final rooftop set down.

Suddenly, the sleigh began to tip.

"Whoa! Steady!" I tried to say in a calm voice, but the reindeer, with Donner in the lead, paid no attention. He had just reached the place where I had practiced the Möbius, and I realized they had started into it. How could they? I hadn't given them any signal. Marcia moaned. I gulped and tried to stop them; they paid no attention.

Out of the corner of my eye I saw Granddad clenching his teeth. There was no choice. I had to do the Möbius, and I *had* to do it right. The first curve, down, and then upside down. I tugged on the reins to pull them right side up again. They paid no attention. We flew along in perfect formation — upside down.

It must have been a half mile before I found the right twitch on the reins to bring the sleigh upright again. Then I turned to head back home. Buck was chortling in the backseat. Granddad looked sick. Marcia never stopped moaning.

I made a decent landing on the roof, then set down in front of the barn. I sat there with a heart so heavy it felt like it was scraping the South

Pole. What could I say? That I'd been fouled by a reindeer who hates me? Yeah. That would sure look good on a Santa Claus résumé.

"Well!" Buck said heartily, "I don't suppose there's any need for Rammer to fly. We all know he can do a better job."

Granddad's lips thinned. "If he doesn't want to fly, he can concede, and Nick will get the job and have the right to name an alternate Santa."

"Hey, hey! No need to get so touchy. Rammer can't wait to fly, can you, son?"

Rammer grumbled something and climbed out of the sleigh. "Can we have lunch first?"

Great. He wanted to have lunch first. I hadn't had breakfast, to avoid being sick during my test. Now I'd have to skip lunch. On the other hand, maybe I should eat a great big meal. What did I care if Rammer was grossed out by my airsick bags. And I'd be sitting next to Buck. That was a bonus.

So I ate everything in sight.

"Do you think that's wise?" Granddad hissed at me when I took my third helping.

"I'm just a passenger this time," I said innocently.

Grandma looked at me sharply, then her lips twitched. "How about some strawberry pie to complete your — mixture?" she asked.

Yeah, strawberry would add just the right touch.

Rammer reversed his route, which was allowed by contest rules. He went for the long section of the flight first. He and April stood whispering for a minute before he climbed in. Maybe she'd given him some advice. Then Rammer gave her the same smile he had at breakfast. They seemed awfully chummy all of a sudden.

Rammer swooped into the air, and my lunch swooped into a bag. When I reached for another bag, Buck scooted as far away from me as he could get.

I got even more airsick than usual. At first I thought it was the big meal, but the longer it went, the more I realized that we were wobbling in the air an awful lot.

"Keep it steady," Granddad kept telling Rammer.

"I am!" But he wasn't.

Marcia was keeping her fingers crossed so hard that her mittens were bunched up tight. But even if Rammer was a little wobbly in the air, it wouldn't make up for me.

Rammer managed a fairly good turn, then headed back for the practice landings. Ten of them. I tried to take ahold of my stomach and wished I hadn't decided to eat lunch.

Swoop. Clunk.

My stomach jumped as the sleigh jolted. I couldn't believe it. Rammer had *missed* the first landing!

Somehow Rammer had managed to bring the sleigh down with only one runner landing on the practice roof. Half the sleigh was hanging off the side. Then with a swish of the reins he took off again. The second time he landed all right, but the next three times the sleigh bounced off the roof, and the automatic safety controls had to kick in to keep us from crashing. Then he put the sleigh into a fast, steep dive and went back for another try.

Granddad suddenly grabbed the reins and roared, "Enough! You lose!" He evened out the sleigh and gently landed. We all climbed out.

Buck looked like a bucket of raw fish had been dumped on top of him. Marcia was doing a victory dance, and Granddad was trying not to smile. But it was Rammer's expression that I was curious about. He didn't look disappointed at all.

"How did it go?" April called as she hurried from the barn.

"Rammer lost!" Buck complained.

"Oh, dear!" she said, but I'm sure the corners of her mouth were edging into a smile. Then she winked at Rammer, and he grinned back at her.

Something was going on, and I was planning on finding out what!

"Okay, what gives?" I demanded from Rammer as we unhitched the sleigh.

"What do you mean?"

"You and I both know that you can fly the sleigh better than that. You lost on purpose."

"Well . . ." He stopped and made a face. "This stuff is okay for a few weeks, and it was fun learning how to fly and all, but I don't want to be Santa Claus forever."

"Then what do you want to do?"

His face lit up as he said, almost reverently, "I want to be an accountant!"

Buck started grumbling about losing the contest as soon as he got inside. "I think we need a rematch," he suggested. "Rammer probably wasn't feeling well."

"He's perfectly all right," April said tartly. "He simply lost. Besides, there are plenty of other things he can do in life, maybe even a few he'd prefer. Not everyone wants to be Santa someday. Just ask Nick about that."

Marcia giggled and I said loudly, "I have an announcement. As the heir, and as the winner of the Santa contest, I am officially designating my sister, Marcia Martin, as the next Santa Claus!"

Everyone clapped, even Buck, after April dug him in the side with her elbow.

My mom says you can choose your friends but not your family. None of us would have chosen Buck Claus for a relative, but he wasn't so bad after April had worked on him for a while. The Claus family came back for a visit in March, and we could almost stand having Buck around.

I still couldn't see Rammer as an accountant, but maybe he'll have asked everyone to call him Steve by then. As long as I didn't have to fly a sleigh anymore, he could call himself anything he liked.

I couldn't blame having Santa Claus in the family for everything. I mean, obnoxious relatives would have shown up anyway. I'd still have four sisters and no brothers. And even without Santa, my parents might have wanted me to do something other than oceanography. I know a lot of people think their family is the weirdest around, so I won't insist that mine is the worst.

But it is the weirdest one that *I* know.